Old Racers, New Racers

by Mary Tillworth

illustrated by the Disney Storybook Art Team

Random House 🏠 New York

Dear Parents:

Congratulations! Your child is taking the first steps on an exciting journey. The destination? Independent reading!

STEP INTO READING® will help your child get there. The program offers five steps to reading success. Each step includes fun stories and colorful art or photographs. In addition to original fiction and books with favorite characters, there are Step into Reading Non-Fiction Readers, Phonics Readers and Boxed Sets, Sticker Readers, and Comic Readers—a complete literacy program with something to interest every child.

Learning to Read, Step by Step!

Ready to Read   Preschool–Kindergarten
• big type and easy words • rhyme and rhythm • picture clues
For children who know the alphabet and are eager to begin reading.

Reading with Help   Preschool–Grade 1
• basic vocabulary • short sentences • simple stories
For children who recognize familiar words and sound out new words with help.

Reading on Your Own   Grades 1–3
• engaging characters • easy-to-follow plots • popular topics
For children who are ready to read on their own.

Reading Paragraphs   Grades 2–3
• challenging vocabulary • short paragraphs • exciting stories
For newly independent readers who read simple sentences with confidence.

Ready for Chapters   Grades 2–4
• chapters • longer paragraphs • full-color art
For children who want to take the plunge into chapter books but still like colorful pictures.

STEP INTO READING® is designed to give every child a successful reading experience. The grade levels are only guides; children will progress through the steps at their own speed, developing confidence in their reading.

Remember, a lifetime love of reading starts with a single step!

Lightning races Storm.

Storm is <u>ahead</u>.

Lightning is <u>behind</u>.

Storm <u>wins</u>
again and again.

Lightning <u>loses</u> again and again.

Cruz is a trainer.
She is <u>up</u>
on a machine.

Lightning is <u>down</u>
on the ground.
Lightning asks Cruz
to help him train.

Lightning and Cruz
are <u>clean</u>.

They enter
a muddy race.
Now they are <u>dirty</u>!

Lightning and Cruz
are <u>small</u>.

Miss Fritter is <u>BIG</u>!

Lightning and Cruz
meet the Legends.

Lightning and Cruz
are <u>new</u>.

The Legends are old.

The Legends help
Lightning train.
Lightning moves slowly.

Lightning moves <u>fast</u>.

But Cruz is faster!

Cruz gets new gear!

Cruz is <u>over</u> Guido.

Guido is <u>under</u> Cruz.

Now Cruz is even faster!

Lightning lets Cruz
race against Storm.
Storm is <u>ahead</u>.
Cruz is <u>behind</u>.

Cruz leaps.
She is
<u>above</u> Storm.

Storm is

below Cruz.

Cruz wins the race!

Cruz jumps <u>high</u>.

Lightning rides <u>low</u>.

Both are winners!